Bantam Books in the Choose Your Own Adventure® Series
Ask your bookseller for the books you have missed

Choose Your Own Adventure® Books for younger readers

THE ABOMINABLE SNOWMAN

BY R.A. MONTGOMERY

ILLUSTRATED BY PAUL GRANGER

BANTAM BOOKS
TORONTO · NEW YORK · LONDON · SYDNEY

RL 4, Age 10 and up

THE ABOMINABLE SNOWMAN

A Bantam Book / May 1982
2nd printing . . . . April 1982   3rd printing . . . . . . August 1982
4th printing . . . . . October 1982

CHOOSE YOUR OWN ADVENTURE®
is a registered trademark of Bantam Books, Inc.,
Registered in U.S. Patent and Trademark Office and elsewhere.

Original conception of Edward Packard

Illustrated by Paul Granger

ISBN 0-553-23332-7

Published simultaneously in the United States and Canada

Bantam Books are published by Bantam Books, Inc. Its trademark, consisting of the words "Bantam Books" and the por-
trayal of a rooster is Registered in U.S. Patent and Trademark
Office and in other countries. Marca Registrada. Bantam
Books, Inc., 666 Fifth Avenue, New York, New York 10103.

PRINTED IN THE UNITED STATES OF AMERICA

O   13 12 11 10 9 8 7 6 5

*This book
is dedicated to
Anson and Ramsey
and to
Roland Palmedo*

WARNING!!!!

Do not read this book straight through from beginning to end. These pages contain many different adventures you can have in the Himalayas as you search for the Abominable Snowman. From time to time as you read along, you will be asked to make decisions and choices.

The adventures you take will be the result of your choices. After you make each choice, follow the instructions to see what happens to you next.

Be careful! Mountaineering can be dangerous. Think before you make a move. You cannot go back. The mountain range is vast. The terrain will often be unexplored. Your expedition will be difficult.

Good luck!

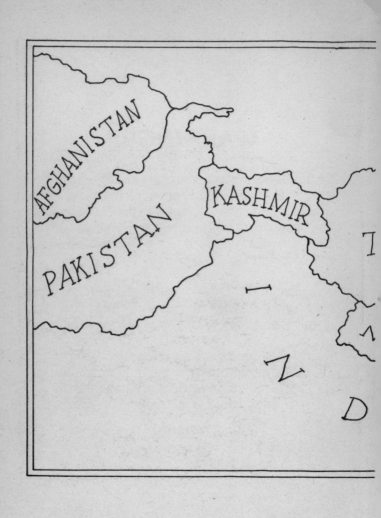

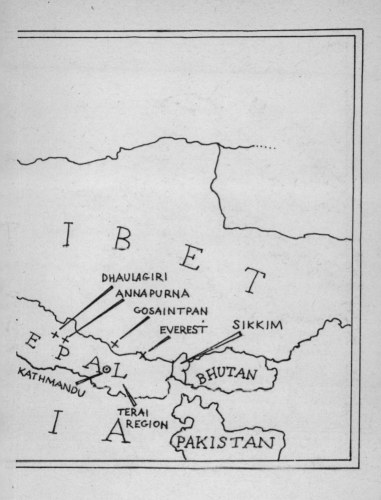

You are a mountain climber. Three years ago you spent the summer at a climbing school in the mountains of Colorado. Your instructors said that you had natural skills as a climber. You made rapid progress, and by the end of the summer you were leading difficult rock and ice climbs.

That summer, you became close friends with a boy named Carlos. The two of you made a good climbing team. Last year you and he were chosen to join an international team. The expedition made it to the top of two unclimbed peaks in South America.

One night on that expedition, the group was seated around the cook tent at the base camp. The expedition leader, Franz, told stories of

climbing in the Himalayas, the highest mountains in the world. They form a great natural wall between India and China, with Nepal tucked in amid the peaks. Everest, K2, and Annapurna are the best-known mountains in the Himalayas. These and many other peaks have been climbed. Still others lie in remote areas where few men have gone. There, said Franz, in the high valleys beneath the snowfields, lives the Yeti, sometimes called the Abominable Snowman.

The Yeti is said to be a huge beast, like a cross between a gorilla and a man. Franz told of how people who have seen the Yeti cannot agree on what it is like. Some say the Yeti is dangerous, ready to carry off the unwary. Others say the Yeti is gentle. The best evidence of the existence of the Yeti is large footprints discovered in the 1950s by a British expedition. No one has ever photographed a Yeti; no one has ever really seen one of these creatures. But the stories persist.

Go on to page 4.

You and Carlos decided then and there to find the Yeti. When you returned from South America, the two of you raised money from the International Foundation For Research Into Strange Phenomena. Your goal: proof positive that Yeti exist. You will find and photograph the Yeti.

And that is what brings you to Kathmandu, the capital of Nepal. Your problems, though, have already begun. Two days ago Carlos left by helicopter to look over the terrain near Mt. Everest. The helicopter returned without him—the pilot told you that Carlos decided to stay up at the Everest base camp for the night, to check out a report that a Yeti had been seen. He had a radio transmitter, but you have received no word from him. The weather turned bad and radio communication was interrupted.

You have written for an appointment to speak with R. N. Runal, the Director of Expeditions and Mountain Research and an authority on the Yeti. You have told him of your plans. You need permits for the expedition and advice and information from Runal.

But what about Carlos?

If you decide to cancel your meeting with Runal and search for Carlos, turn to page 5.

If you feel that Carlos is OK and go ahead with your plan to meet Runal, turn to page 6.

You telephone Mr. Runal at the Foreign Ministry and tell him that you are worried about Carlos and that you want to search for him.

"Of course. I understand. Please allow me the honor of coming with you. I could be of help."

You gladly accept the help of Mr. Runal. His reputation as a mountaineer is excellent. He is able to arrange for a Royal Nepalese Army helicopter to meet you at the Tribuhavan airport.

Two hours later you land at the Everest base camp where Carlos was last seen. His red nylon mountain tent is still there, but the storm has erased all footprints.

Runal tells you that in most of the stories about Yeti, the creatures are well below here. Yet recent reports tell of Yeti up in the glaciers.

If you and Runal search below the base camp in the valley, turn to page 8.

If you go above the base camp, turn to page 10.

You walk down a street bordered by tall pines. They are green-blue, and the branches and needles are very fine and delicate. Hanging from the upper branches are what look like huge, tear-shaped, blackish-brown fruit. You stop and look up, wondering what they are. Then one moves, spreads giant wings, and flaps off. They are bats, the largest bats you have ever seen!

You reach the Foreign Ministry, and you are shown to a waiting room. You wait a few minutes and then are ushered in to meet R. N. Runal, Director of Expeditions and Mountain Research for the Nepalese government.

"Welcome to our country. We wish you success. But I have some bad news. The expedition you have proposed could be very dangerous."

You look at him, not knowing what to expect.

Go on to page 7.

"Recently, a large expedition set out without telling us that they were going after the Yeti," says Runal. "They used guns and traps, and tried to kill one of them. The Yeti are angry."

You interrupt him by saying, "Mr. Runal, we just want to find a Yeti. We have no intention of ever hurting a Yeti."

"I know that. We have checked up on you. It is a shame about the others. I must advise against going into Yeti territory. I could arrange a trip for you into the Terai region, out of the mountains, in the jungle area. You could photograph and study the tigers. They are famous, and also dangerous. Later, perhaps, you could conduct the expedition you are leading."

If you decide to go ahead with the expedition for the Yeti, turn to page 13.

If you decide to postpone the expedition to let the Yeti calm down and go on to the Terai region in search of tigers, turn to page 15.

The helicopter stays at base camp, and you and Runal descend on foot along a narrow, rocky path below the snow line into a pine forest.

The trail suddenly becomes very steep, and one side falls off more than a thousand meters to a river gorge. You come to a small stone house with a thatched roof. An old woman sits in the sunlight by the door.

"Can you tell us if any climbers came by here? My friend is about five foot nine, medium build, has dark hair." Runal translates your description into Nepali.

The woman nods, and says two men came by. The younger one left a note:

> Don't follow.
> Wait at base camp.
> *Carlos*

Runal turns to you with a puzzled look on his face.

"Carlos is your friend. If it were up to me, I would ignore his message. But you know him better. What now? What do you think?"

If you obey the message and climb back up to the base camp to wait for Carlos, turn to page 18.

If you ignore the message and decide to look for Carlos, turn to page 14.

Above the base camp are the dangerous "seracs." These huge blocks of ice are always moving, and people threading their way through this maze of ice are in constant danger. Runal leads the way. You both have attached the climbing spikes called crampons to your boots, and are attached to each other by a slender nylon rope.

"Watch out! Jump!"

A block of ice quivers and tumbles to the side, sending clouds of snow and ice crystals in the air. Runal had seen it just in time. You move more slowly now, careful not to get near these treacherous seracs.

Then, going around a serac as large as a two-story house, you find him. Carlos is sitting in the sun, fidgeting with his camera.

"Hey, what are you guys doing here?"

"That's what we want to know. You scared us to death with your disappearing act. What's up?"

Carlos puts the camera away and, after you introduce him to Runal, explains that he found tracks, Yeti tracks perhaps, and followed them. He tried to radio, but the weather blocked it. The tracks faded, and he couldn't find his way back to the camp. He had been sitting and waiting. Runal examines one track protected from drifting snow, and explains that they are blue bear tracks and not Yeti tracks.

So, disappointed, you go back to the copter and return to Kathmandu.

Go on to page 12.

The next day you go to the shop of Sirdar Podang Sorba, a well-known Sherpa guide. Carlos stays with Runal, getting the permits.

You enter the store and there, behind a counter stacked with dried food in plastic bags, tanks of gas for mountain stoves, and wool hats, is Sirdar Sorba. You introduce yourself, and immediately you like this man. He is warm and friendly, and he has been with the Japanese expedition to Pumori and a French Everest attempt.

Maybe you should ask him to join you as you search for the Yeti.

If you ask Sirdar to come along in your expedition, turn to page 22.

If you wait and decide to talk it over with Carlos, turn to page 21.

"I appreciate your warning and kind offer of the alternative to go to the Terai," you say. "We are committed to this expedition. We will search for the Yeti with openness and friendship."

R. N. Runal nods his head and speaks quickly to his assistant in Nepali. Within minutes you have the necessary papers for the expedition, stamped in the proper places with the official seal of the Nepalese government. As you shake hands before leaving, he stops you. "If you are determined to go on your expedition, it could be easier and safer if I come with you."

What should you do?

If you accept Runal's offer to join you, turn to page 23.

If you decline his offer, turn to page 25.

"Carlos may be in trouble. We must find him."

Runal nods in agreement, and then he gives the woman two copper rupees. She smiles at him and speaks quickly in Nepali. Then she shuffles into the house. You and Runal remain outside, next to the small garden where cucumbers and squash lie ripening.

"What was that all about? What did the old woman say?" You adjust your rucksack straps to stop them from chafing your shoulders.

Runal looks at you and says, "The woman claims that your friend was traveling with a Yeti."

You stare at Runal in disbelief. But why not? You are here to find them; maybe *they* found *you* this time.

You head down the trail not knowing quite what to expect.

Turn to page 32.

You talk with Runal at length about the Terai, a tropical zone at sea level just one hundred miles from Everest, the highest elevation on earth. What contrast! You realize that it will make excellent material for a feature article for your local paper.

"The Terai is incredible," Runal tells you. "The jungle is filled with flowers and animals, the fierce Indian tiger, and the dangerous rhinoceros. I will arrange to have elephants carry you into the remote areas."

Within two days, after leaving a message for Carlos, you are riding on an elephant's back, swaying with its ponderous footsteps.

The heat is almost unbearable, and drops of sweat roll down your neck and soak your khaki safari shirt.

You come to a stream bordered by thick green jungle. There, in the sand, are the prints of many boots. Also in the sand are spent cartridges from a heavy-caliber weapon.

"Not good. Not good. Must be poachers after tiger skins and elephant tusks. Dangerous," says your guide.

"Let's follow them. Let's see what they're up to."

"OK, but maybe we should split up; that way we can cover more territory."

Go on to the next page.

If you split up, turn to page 26.

If you stay together, turn to page 28.

You hesitate and then say that it would be best to return to the base camp. However, it is getting late, and the trail back up will be especially dangerous at night. Runal suggests that it would be better to stay right where you are until morning.

You make arrangements with the woman to spend the night. She brings a simple meal of rice, squash, and buttered tea. You are very nervous, but you trust Carlos's judgment. Whatever is going on is out of your hands for now, anyway.

You can't sleep, and the wind of the high mountains keeps you restless and heightens your worry.

Close to dawn, you hear a high, piercing scream.

Turn to page 31.

You're quick, but not quick enough. Sirdar drops the ax and pulls both your arms behind your back.

The two men who were in the doorway are now inside the store. One of them shuts the door and bolts it. The click of the bolt, locking you in and help out, is very ominous.

The three men surround you. Sirdar says, "Foolish one. Now you have gone too far. Why are you here? What do you want?"

The man with the beard fondles a small, ugly-looking automatic pistol.

"I meant no harm. I just wanted to see what was inside the pocket."

"Well, there's no way out. We need both of you for our plan. You will send a message to your friend, telling him you've found an important clue. Get him to come here. If you don't, we'll kill you on the spot. If you do as we say, well, maybe you'll live. We'll have to see. We've been following you guys. We thought we would use you to get this stuff out of the country." He points at packages wrapped in brown paper. It's probably hashish, you think. What an awful position to be in. What do you do now?

If you say you'll write the note to Carlos, turn to page 47.

If you refuse, turn to page 48.

You think Carlos should have a chance to meet Sirdar. You occupy yourself with buying the high altitude tents, ice axes, crampons, ropes, the rock spikes called pitons, and ice screws.

While looking through a rack of down-filled parkas used on previous mountain expeditions, you come across one that attracts your attention. It is a purple parka, medium-sized, but what is so interesting about it is that one of the pockets bulges.

You give a quick look around the shop to make sure that no one is watching. You undo the zipper. It feels like there's a rock in the pocket. You take it out and unwrap the heavy brown paper that covers it. There in your hand is a fragment of a skull! It is yellowed with age. Could this be a Yeti skull? Yikes! It is spooky to hold the thing.

You examine a piece of paper that is stuffed inside the skull. It is the sort of rice paper used for tracings and for art work. It's a map, and it shows a road leading from Kathmandu to the town of Nagarkot. The word "Treasure" appears over an X next to an abandoned temple of the Hindu god Shiva.

Turn to page 34.

"How about joining us on our search for the Yeti, Sirdar?"

He smiles and hesitates. Then he picks up two sticks of incense. One is longer than the other. He lights them both, and their rich fragrance fills the air of his small store.

"You see, as one fragrance merges with the other we do not know the difference between them. Only when the shorter stick burns out will we know which stick was the fragrance of rose and which was the fragrance of magnolia."

You are puzzled by his talk of incense. You ask, "So, what does that mean, Sirdar?"

"It does not mean anything, it only IS."

You are really confused now. What to do? Perhaps you should leave this talk of incense alone and forget about asking Sirdar to join you. Maybe he is crazy.

If you back out of the offer to take him on the expedition, turn to page 38.

If you persist and try to understand his point, turn to page 39.

Now that he is a member of your expedition, Runal sends out a government team to set up your base camp and find Carlos. In a few days Carlos has rejoined you, and all three of you are out on the trail. Runal turns out to be a wonderful companion. Six porters carry your food and tents and supplies. This leaves you free to explore the steep valley sides and the small villages along the way.

The days are long. You begin at first light and go on until six in the evening. Your legs ache from the constant pounding as you walk along the narrow trails which have served these Nepalese people for hundreds of years. Above you are bright blue skies dotted with clouds. The snow and ice flanks of Lhotse, Pumori, and Everest rise above the green of the lower slopes.

Go on to page 24.

As you approach a village, Runal points out a large building with a red roof, which stands above the small, neat houses clustered about it.

"That is the monastery where there lives a monk, a Buddhist monk, who has seen and lived with the Yeti."

"But I thought no one had really seen one. I thought no one alive had spent time with the Yeti."

Runal answers, "It is a well-kept secret. Those who share the secret knowledge of the Yeti are pledged to reveal this knowledge only to appointed people. You, and you alone, are one of the appointed. It has been seen in the stars; it has been read in your hand."

"What do you mean? Who saw it in the stars? Who read it in my hand?"

Runal does not answer for several minutes. Then he speaks. "If you accept the secret knowledge, your life will change. You will never be the same. Decide now."

If you are ready for the secret knowledge of the Yeti, and the responsibility that goes with it, turn to page 41.

If you reject the offer of secret knowledge, turn to page 116.

"I think we'll go it alone. But thanks, anyway."

Mr. Runal shakes your hand, but he does not smile. It is clear that you have offended this man.

What should you do? Is an apology in order? Should you try to patch things up?

If you try to make amends and end up inviting him to accompany you, turn to page 42.

If you stick to your decision, turn to page 43.

"OK," you say to the guide, "you go on downstream. I'll head into the jungle and circle around, and meet you at the stream in three hours. If you need help, fire three shots, wait six seconds, and fire three more shots."

"OK. Be careful."

You set off into the jungle, moving as quietly as possible. Two hours later you stop for a rest, swatting at the mosquitoes and picking off the leeches. With a roar, a magnificent tiger, at least eight feet in length from nose to tail, springs out of the brush.

You are finished.

The End

You and your guide head downstream. You find the poachers. Killing tigers and elephants for their skins and tusks is a serious crime in Nepal. They don't believe in leaving evidence of their actvities. You try running away into the forest, but the poachers are quick. They don't leave any witnesses.

The End

"Yeeeeeowee!"

The noise seems to be coming from right outside your window. Runal moves quickly to the doorway. The woman is outside the house at the edge of the trail, holding up a battered kerosene lantern.

You hear the cry again. This time it is even louder.

"Yeoweee!! Yi, Yi, Yeeeoweee!!"

Suddenly the sound diminishes. It seems to be going farther and farther away. The woman waves her lantern. Is it a signal, or is she trying to frighten whatever it was away?

"Those are the Yeti," she says. "They invite you to join them and your friend Carlos."

What should you do? This is more than you had bargained for.

You look at Runal, and then at the woman. It is chilly in the half-light of morning. The Yeti sound is growing fainter by the minute.

If you follow after the sound of the Yeti, turn to page 46.

If you return to the base camp and the helicopter, turn to page 45.

As you race down the path you see a few footprints that might have been left by a Yeti. Suddenly it is very quiet. The birds have stopped singing. The only sound you hear is your footsteps and Runal's right behind you. You wonder why.

It doesn't take long to find out. Around a curve in the path you run smack into a band of creatures that can only be Yeti. They are aiming an ancient bronze cannon at you. One of them touches a light to the fuse.

And that is the last thing you remember.

The End

You know that this is too exciting for you to wait for Carlos. You must find out more about it immediately. You walk over to the counter and ask Sirdar where the parka came from.

Sirdar looks up in surprise. There is fear in his eyes when he sees you holding up the purple parka.

"Oh, that is not for sale. That is a mistake to have it there. Please give it to me. Give it to me."

You look in the parka and there, near the collar, is Sirdar's name stenciled in black ink. You look up and see Sirdar moving toward you with an ice ax in his hand. He raises the ice ax as though to strike.

You throw the parka at him. It is just enough to startle him for a second. You run for the door but standing there are two tough-looking men. They are Westerners. One has a beard, and the other is clean-shaven, but his hair hangs down to his shoulders. You are just about cornered. You jump to the right, duck to the left, and make for the rack of ice axes at the back of the shop.

Turn to page 19.

36

Run! You run for your life! You dash for the trees at the edge of the cliff. Maybe you can hide there. But the Yeti is fast, faster than you ever thought.

Then you are falling, slipping into space over the cliff. But miraculously, the Yeti reaches out and grabs you, saving you just in time from certain death. He carries you back to your tent, puts you down gently, and slips off into the night.

The End

"I don't think I understand. Before you come with us, I'd better talk with my partner. He's not far away. I'll go find him now. If I don't come back, don't wait for me."

You start slowly toward the door when the incense smoke gets very thick. In an instant it is so thick that you can't find the door. You wander around in the smoke for a long time, until you regret having changed your mind about taking Sirdar with you. By then it is too late. You never find the door, or anything else.

The End

"OK, so you want me to choose which stick is rose and which is magnolia. Is that it? Is it a test? If I'm right you'll go, if not you won't?"

Sirdar smiles, displaying gold caps on three of his upper front teeth. He nods his head.

"Here goes," you say. "The longer stick is Kashmiri Rose incense."

Sirdar claps his hands, brings them up to his forehead, and bows slightly, saying, "Namaste, bara sahib. I am at your command, Master."

It is decided. He will accompany you. You have chosen the right one.

Some things just happen by chance. This was one of them. You ask, "Where should we head? Annapurna or the Lhotse-Everest region? What do you think, Sirdar?"

"Many have seen Yeti prints near Everest, but there is the region near Annapurna and Macha-puchhre (Fish Tail Mountain), where we could have good luck. The Everest region has been more fully explored; Annapurna is less well known."

If you choose the Annapurna region, turn to page 51.

If you choose the Everest region, turn to page 49.

"I gladly accept your offer. I am ready for the knowledge."

"Come with me." He leads you to the monastery. Carlos stays behind.

You and Runal enter the monastery through a huge wooden door. It is very dark inside, but you make out the figure of an old man seated on the floor. Behind him is a statue of Buddha. The man welcomes you and motions you to sit before him. You see that he is wearing the robes of a monk. You are served yak-butter tea, a thick broth that you find hard to swallow.

"Listen well with heart, head, and body. Listen with eyes more than with ears. Heed the cry of the Yeti," the old monk tells you.

You can hear bells in the distance, and wind in the pine trees just outside the window. It is beautiful.

You sit for what seems like hours, listening with your whole being.

Finally, the monk speaks.

"Time now to go on the next journey."

If you agree to take the journey, turn to page 52.

If you decide that you are not prepared to change your life forever, turn to page 61.

"Mr. Runal, I beg your pardon, sir. I have made a mistake. This is your country, and we need your help. Please do accompany us. It will be our honor and pleasure to have you with us."

The room is silent. You shift nervously and stare out the window at the palace grounds and the formal gardens.

Runal does not respond right away. He fiddles with a pencil on his desk, deep in thought.

"I appreciate the kind offer. I can only accept if you allow me the great honor of being expedition leader. If you will allow this, I may be able to arrange for funds from the government, as well as tactical support from the Royal Nepalese Army, including helicopters."

This catches you by surprise. You are the leader.

*If you allow him to be expedition leader,
turn to page 54.*

*If you point out that that will not be possible,
turn to page 55.*

You leave Runal's office. As you walk outside you are hit with torrential rain. It falls from the sky, hitting the earth in explosive drops. You planned your expedition assuming the monsoons would be over by now, but apparently they are not.

You sit it out in your hotel for three weeks. The constant rain has closed off the trails to the mountain valleys with mud slides and boulders. Nature has gone wild and your expedition is blocked for good. Too bad.

The End

"We've got to get back up to the base camp," you say.

Runal grabs your arm. "I know that cry. It is the battle cry, the cry of anger and revenge. We'll get help and come back for Carlos."

You are almost out of breath as you hurry up the trail, but you ask why the Yeti are angry.

"Too many people have sought them out, hunted them, tormented them. They have had enough."

The trail seems much steeper than you had remembered. Then you are at the edge of the glacier where the camp was pitched. The light of the late morning sun almost blinds you as it flashes off the ice.

The helicopter lies smashed in the snow. The rotor blades are twisted and the Plexiglas is shattered. There is no sign of the pilot, just giant footprints—Yeti footprints, leading off to the heart of the icefall.

If you follow the prints, turn to page 56.

If you stay where you are, hoping for help, turn to page 57.

You start to run down the trail. Runal follows you.

Soon you come to an abrupt halt. There in front of you is the body of a yak, the ox of the high mountains. Its horns have been savagely twisted off. They are now used as markers to point the way from the path to a thick rhododendron-and-pine grove.

You pause, looking at the horrible sight of the dead yak. The horns may be pointing you to Carlos, or they may lead into a trap.

If you take Runal with you into the grove for added protection, turn to page 58.

If you leave Runal behind as a rear guard, because one person can move more quietly and quickly, and go into the grove by yourself, turn to page 60.

"I'll get Carlos here. I'm not sure where he is, though," you say.

The muzzle of the automatic wavers, points at you, and then the man holding the gun lowers it and slips it into his pocket. For the time being it looks as though the danger is over.

How can you get out of luring Carlos into this trap? Then you remember a special signal you used when climbing with ropes. Three sharp tugs on the rope meant trouble.

"Okay, give me pen and paper." They hand you these things and you begin to write.

"Hey, this pen doesn't work. Look!"

You quickly scratch three lines on the paper with the pen. Of course it works, and you say, "Well, I guess it's working now."

You hope that the three marks are enough to warn Carlos. You need time to plan your escape.

The bearded man speaks in a German accent. "Tell us now what you know about the map."

*If you make up a fantastic story,
turn to page 63.*

*If you insist that you know nothing,
turn to page 64.*

"Never, never. I'm not falling for your stuff. If you want Carlos, then go after him yourself."

At that very moment there is a loud knock on the door.

"Open up. Police. You're surrounded." The door crashes open and three Nepalese soldiers and a police officer rush in. Carlos is behind them.

The officer nods at them and says, "Hands up. Well, well, we finally got you, didn't we? It's jail for you. Smugglers are all the same. Fortunately, we have been following you for the last three weeks. When you started following these two, we followed them also. Carlos has helped us. Your smuggling days are over."

You are badly shaken, but the Nepalese government now considers you and Carlos heroes, and they will give you all the help you need for your expedition.

The End

Two days later, with permits obtained and supplies bought, you, Carlos, and Sirdar start the long journey from Kathmandu to Pokhara.

Three days after that, you and your party, along with twelve porters to carry the supplies, are camped out in a field high above the valley floor near a small village called Dhumpus.

That night, after a dinner of brown rice and lentils, onions, and garlic, you sit in front of your red mountain tents watching the moon play on the snowy white flanks of Annapurna and Dhaulagiri. It is nearly silent, and cool. You are tired from the climb, but very glad to be there. With the darkened village behind you, you feel as though your group might be the only people on Earth.

Then you see a light flash on Annapurna. Then it repeats. It flashes again. It may just be a reflection, or another party, or it may be a signal from someone in trouble—or from the Yeti.

If you think it is a signal, turn to page 65.

If you think it is just another climbing party, turn to page 67.

Runal is still with you. He taps you on the shoulder, and you rise and follow him to the back of the monastery, behind the golden Buddha. The heavy smell of rose-scented incense fills the air.

"The Yeti are guides to Shangri-La. They take the chosen people to this hidden valley, which many have heard of and only a few have seen."

You nod, wondering what comes next.

"One last chance, my friend. Turn back now and live a normal life with your friend Carlos. Go ahead and accept the life of the secret world."

If you go on, turn to page 70.

If you turn back, turn to page 72.

"OK, Mr. Runal, you may lead the expedition. I am sure that our goals are the same, and we can use the extra support from your government."

Runal's connections within the government turn out to be very useful. Soon the expedition has better supplies and equipment than you would have been able to get on your own. His knowledge about the Yeti proves to be useful, and you are already learning more about them.

He makes arrangements for you to be carried by helicopter to the base camp at Mt. Everest. Maybe it's the best to have him lead. It's his land, and he knows it well.

Turn to page 23.

The telephone rings, breaking the silence in the room. Runal excuses himself and picks it up.

"Yes. Yes. I understand. . . . I will tell them."

He turns to you with a serious look on his face. "Our king is bothered that people are disturbing the peace of our land. He apologizes, but he has decided to close the mountains to all expeditions. It is time for a rest. The Yeti are not animals. We will not allow them to be hunted any more. I am sorry, my friend."

Well, at least you didn't have to refuse Runal's offer of leadership.

The End

56

The prints lead you into the intricate maze of the icefall. You walk very carefully, because even the slightest movement of the glacier could start a trembling and a moving of the ice blocks. Then, abruptly, the footprints stop. They just stop, as if the owners of the feet suddenly sprouted wings and flew away.

You look all around at the shimmering ice, at the compacted snow, at the sharp gray and brown of rock flanked by ice. Overhead, several enormous birds soar in the rising currents of air. On the summit of the mountains, curls of snow looking like smoke rise in the gathering wind.

You and Runal stand in awe of the mountains, momentarily forgetting your mission.

Then something catches your eye. It is a piece of red nylon cloth held down by a small chunk of ice. Could it be Carlos's tent? You investigate and, as you stoop to pick it up, you hear a sudden noise.

Turn to page 73.

You stay near the remains of the camp, following Carlos's instructions. Runal agrees that this is correct.

"You see, my friend, the high mountains, this roof of the world, they hold secrets, mysteries, dangers. We have trespassed. We should wait and see what happens."

You wait for a while, but you decide that you have to do something to save Carlos. Maybe the old woman lied. Maybe she made up the story about Carlos being with the Yeti. Maybe the weird cries were some kind of temple horn down in the valley. Maybe it was phony. But why? You are confused.

"Runal, I'm going back down after Carlos. You stay here if you wish. I can't leave him."

Runal agrees, but he stays to wait for a search helicopter.

Turn to page 77.

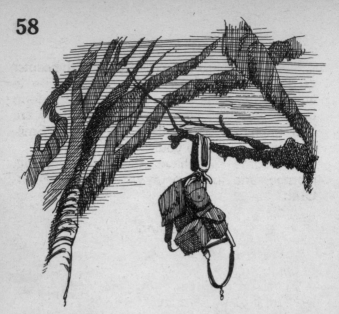

Cautiously, you and Runal enter the grove. The pale light of dawn does little to illuminate this eerie place. You are both careful not to make noise.

Runal tugs at your sleeve. He points above and ahead, into the branches of a pine. Hanging from the branches is a red backpack. You approach cautiously. It looks like the pack that Carlos had been carrying. It may have been taken from him, or he might have left it as a warning.

If you retreat now and go for more help, turn to page 79.

If you give the special birdcall whistle that you and Carlos use as your emergency code, turn to page 80.

In a domed room, you see Carlos in the center of a group of people. While you look on in amazement, some of the people change form before your very eyes. One moment they are Yeti, the next unicorns, the next buddhas. Smiling, Carlos speaks to you.

"Welcome. You have completed a difficult journey, and found your way to Heaven-on-Earth."

The End

You ask yourself why you are doing this. Who knows what's in there? But Carlos is in danger, so you enter the thicket. The pale light barely penetrates the pine trees. After fifteen minutes of very slow progress, you come across a strange-looking fence. It seems to be made of some kind of aluminum or stainless steel.

You test it, and the hinges allow a gate to swing back. Peculiar that it was not locked. Again you peer about, but no one is there. You follow a well-worn path that leads to a rock face. At the base of the rock face, you find a strange carving.

A bright red door leads into the rock wall, and a path leads away from the wall. What now?

If you enter the door, turn to page 82.

If you follow the path, turn to page 81.

. You get up and head for the door. But you can't walk out. An invisible barrier stops you. The monk smiles at you. Perhaps he understands your feelings of conflict.

"I'm not too happy being here. I'm frightened."

The monk says, "Nothing is easy; many things are frightening. If you must leave, then leave; you will return when you are ready."

You thank the monk. This time nothing blocks you from going through the door. Several minutes later you look back, not knowing whether you made the right choice or not.

The End

"Well, you see, it's like this. I am the prince of a tribe of superior beings from the lost continent of Atlantis. We live under the sea off the coast of Africa. Now we are ready to join forces with the Yeti—a tribe from the planet Borodoz which has been in the high mountains for the last three hundred years."

The three look at you and begin to laugh. One of them says, "Sure, and I'm Julius Caesar, and here is Cleopatra." They all laugh at the big joke. This gives you time to whip out your Swiss Army knife. You cut some cords hanging from the ceiling. A mountain tent on display falls down on top of your enemies. You scoot out the door just in time.

You forget about supplies for now, and go to the police.

The End

"I know nothing, nothing."

The bearded one scowls and says, "That's what they all say. Let's end it right here. That expedition for the Yeti is phony. They're all from Interpol."

"Hey, I'll make a deal." You don't have the faintest idea what kind of a "deal" you could offer, but you need to stall for time. Then, to your immense surprise, Sirdar opens the back door. In troop six men. They are all holding weapons.

"Gentlemen, you are under arrest." He flashes a badge and smiles at you. "Sorry, my friend. You just came here at the wrong time. I had to attack you to keep these men from becoming suspicious. The map you found will lead us to their hidden supplies. Good luck on your expedition."

The End

"Carlos, look at that flashing light!" Once again the light blinks three times, then stops. Then it blinks again. "What do you think? Could be trouble."

Sirdar says, "That could be a disaster signal. But it is very far from here, across the valley and just below the glacier. We could go, or I could return to Pokhara and report it to the authorities."

"How much time would it take you to get back to Pokhara?"

"I can go faster than our whole group. Perhaps it would take a day, and they would send a helicopter. Without outside help, there is little we could do if there is someone in trouble. But they may need help quickly."

Should you respond to the call for help? If so, turn to page 84.

If you decide to let Sirdar return to Pokhara for help, turn to page 85.

"Let's watch it. I'm not sure that it's anything more than someone playing with a flashlight."

For the next two hours you sit and watch the spot where the flashes came from. But the flashing has stopped. It's cold now, and you are glad to have your parkas. The stars are bright, and you are awed by the immensity of the mountains before you. No wonder so many people have been attracted to them.

You turn in, tired from the long hike and anxious to get on with the search for the Yeti.

Four hours later, at about 2 A.M., you are awakened by a wailing noise near your tent.

Yeeeeeeeeee Ah, Ah, Ah!!

Yeeeeeeeeee Ah, Ah, Ah!!!!

You unzip the tent flap and peer out into the darkness.

There, near the pile of gear, is a dark mass. Maybe it's a Yeti. You reach for your camera. Maybe you can get a picture.

Then the mass rears up and lurches for the tents where Carlos and Sirdar are sleeping.

What should you do? If you want to click the picture, turn to page 86.

If you decide instead to grab an ice ax and try to frighten this creature, turn to page 87.

"Tonight we stay in the house of a friend. We must rest, and get used to the thin air." Sirdar leads the way to a group of houses made of stone. They are simple, lovely houses. On the small porches men, women, and children sit drinking tea. Chickens scratch at tufts of grass. High above, black birds with wingspans of nearly three meters soar on the rising air currents. At one end of the village are several thin poles with long, narrow prayer flags snaking in the light wind.

At all times you are aware of the immensity of the mountains. You have never been anywhere quite so silent, either.

For three days you stay in this small village, taking short walks, testing your legs and lungs at this high altitude. On the afternoon of the third day, Sirdar tells you that you are ready. "You are all strong. Your hearts have slowed down now. Your breathing is much better. We are ready to do the hard climbing at this altitude. We must hurry now. I have reports that the Yeti have been active in the Khumbu Icefall at Everest."

Go on to page 69.

He pauses and looks first at you, and then at Carlos. "It is long and hard and dangerous in the icefall. Great pieces of ice tumble from the glacier and pile up like children's building blocks. The ice may crack and give way when you least suspect. Many have died in these icefalls. You don't know which way to turn. Suddenly, great cracks open about you. Without warning, tons of ice come down upon you. Perhaps that is why the Yeti like the icefall. Few people will risk going there."

You understand the danger. It is well known that these regions have taken many lives. You had hoped that you could avoid the dangers of the Khumbu Icefall. But such recent sightings of the Yeti are tempting. What should you do?

If you take the risks, turn to page 88.

If you can't decide, turn to page 89.

"I am ready, Runal. Lead the way."

Runal taps three times on the back of the buddha, near the spot where its skull and neck join. It makes a clanging sound, as if cymbals are being struck.

Wow! Before you stands a creature who is seven feet tall, with broad shoulders and huge feet. His face is gentle and kind. You are not frightened.

You turn to Runal. He smiles and says, "This is Zodak. He is your own special guide. Follow him. He will take you where you must go."

"Can I say goodbye to Carlos?"

"It is not usual. I do not advise it; it might upset him and you. But if you wish, go and say farewell."

*If you do and bid farewell to Carlos,
turn to page 90.*

*If you decide against bidding farewell,
turn to page 91.*

Secret worlds. This is all too scary.

To your way of thinking, you are not yet ready for this kind of thing. You want to explore the world you live in right now. Maybe Runal is crazy. Maybe he is a kidnapper. You will never know.

You can walk out of the monastery, find Carlos, and continue the expedition.

That's what you came halfway around the world for, and that's what you intend to do. You collect Carlos from in front of the monastery and continue your search for the Yeti.

The End

From behind huge blocks of ice dart four Yeti. You and Runal are captured immediately. The Yeti's strength is unbelievable. Your arms are held in viselike grips. They carry you like sacks of rice, up further into the icefall. Finally, you are put down, and there in front of you is the helicopter pilot. He is unharmed. One of the Yeti speaks.

Turn to page 74, then 75, then 76.

"Well, thank you for coming here. We thought it would be nice to study you, and it would have been hard for us to travel to your country." The Yeti laughs a low, long chuckle. The others grin. You look at Runal, at the helicopter pilot, at the surrounding mountains.

The Yeti continues, "Your friend is safe. He will be brought back to you later. Now we have had enough of you, and we hope you have had enough of us." The Yeti walk off and disappear into the icefall.

You find your way back to the smashed helicopter. Carlos is there, unharmed as they said. Your only disappointment is at not getting a picture.

The End

You start down the trail, and right before your eyes a round orange-colored mass appears. It hovers near you. It is about the size of a beach ball.

ZAP! You are hit by a light beam. It feels as though you are being bathed in warm salt water. It is rather pleasant, and removes all fear. You don't want to run or hide from this creature, whatever it is.

"Hey, it's OK. I'm not your enemy. I'm not bad. Who are you, or—or I mean, what are you?" You stand still, and several more of these round, glowing blobs gather round you.

"Earthling wishes knowledge. Earthling friendly. Release light beam. Sensor indicates Earthling is honest and speaks only truth."

The light beam switches off, and in a way you miss the comfort of its warmth. "I wish Carlos were here," you say, "so he could see what is going on." You really wish he were with you.

Then before your eyes Carlos appears! "Carlos! What's up? Where did you come from? This is weird."

Turn to page 78.

Carlos smiles at you. "My friend, your wish was granted. That's the way it is with these Movidians. If they like you and believe in you, then your thoughts and wishes become real. I've been with them for the last two days. Up here in the mountains, things seem really clear and easy to understand. These mechanical creatures, well, they are higher beings. They use the mountains as their Earth base."

There is a humming sound, almost like cats purring. It is coming from the three creatures that Carlos calls Movidians.

One speaks again in a high, mechanical-sounding voice.

"Time now for decision. We invite you to come with us to the Planet of the Seas in the Void of the Seven Moons. Will you come?"

If you go, turn to page 100.

If you refuse, explaining your mission to search for the Yeti, turn to page 102.

"Let's go back!"

Runal nods his agreement. This looks too much like a trap. You believe that Carlos left his pack as a warning to you.

Just as you slip out of the thicket, you see a huge creature, seven or more feet tall, weighing at least two hundred pounds, with short reddish fur covering its body. The creature has an oval, pointed head. Its feet are very wide and long. It sits next to the dead yak, eating.

You are nearly paralyzed with fear. But this may be your only chance to get a photograph!

If you take pictures, turn to page 92.

If you retreat into the thicket, turn to page 94.

"Too wheeet, too wheeet, too tooooo."

You have trouble whistling, you are so nervous. Then you repeat the signal, only louder this time.

"Too wheeet, too wheeet, too tooooo."

There is a sudden crackling of bushes and twigs. You and Runal pull back, ready to run for it. Then Carlos breaks out of the brush, sees you two, and yells, "Run for it, run for it!"

A camera dangles from his neck, and the three of you dart out of the thicket and make for the trail. You keep on going until you can go no further. Between gasps for breath, Carlos tells you that the Yeti carried him to the thicket and allowed him to photograph a group of sixteen Yeti. They told him that now he had what he needed, and that they wanted to be left alone.

"Well, why were we invited?" you ask.

"To help me get back, I guess. I had no idea where I was."

You all go back to the helicopter, and return to Kathmandu with the first pictures the world has ever seen of the Yeti.

The End

The door is too scary. Who knows what is behind it? The path, at least, is in the open. You scan the rock face, give one last look at the door, and edge off onto the path.

Within fifty paces you are up against a steep rock cliff. There seems to be no way out. Behind you the path seems to disappear into a maze of trees. Then you hear the high-pitched call of the Yeti, loud and mocking.

A crackling sound makes you look up. You see a huge avalanche of ice and snow thundering down at you from high above.

Turn to page 110.

With your heart thumping so hard you believe the whole world can hear it, you push the red door open. Inside is a tunnel with smooth walls, illuminated by a gentle rose-colored light. There seems to be no sign of life.

The tunnel winds on for some meters, and then ends abruptly. You find yourself standing in a long, narrow valley with steep walls leading to high, snow-covered peaks, probably Lhotse and Pumori from the look of them. The valley is warm, filled with flowering plants and trees, well guarded from strong winds.

A boy of eight or nine sits on a carved bench. He smiles at you and says in English, "Welcome. We thought you would come. Your friend Carlos is anxious to see you."

"Where is Carlos?"

"Oh, not far. But if you wish to join him, you must agree never to go back to the world you came from. Do you understand?"

If you want to join Carlos, turn to page 97.

If you decide to leave, turn to page 93.

It takes you most of the night to thread your way down steep, tricky trails to reach the valley floor. Once there, you start up the immense Annapurna, scrambling over rocks and skirting the glacier. It is cold, and the night seems long to the three of you.

Several more times you see flickers of light. Now you are sure you have done the right thing. Someone needs help.

Near noon, Carlos says, "Stop. I think I see something."

Then before your eyes, you see what you had come for. A small fire burns between great boulders. Dancing around the fire are eleven Yeti. You have stumbled into a Yeti celebration at the end of the monsoons. You quietly watch, taking pictures and making notes. You have proved, at last, that the Yeti really exist.

The End

"You go ahead, Sirdar. We'll stay here and keep watch."

He vanishes into the dark night. There is no wind, only the silence of mountains and sky and stars. Somewhere in the distance you hear the rumbling sound of water as it flows and drops from the glaciers that embrace Annapurna.

Carlos says, "We should go and help them. I feel selfish, sitting here safe and sound."

So near dawn you set off without your guide. The going is rough, and you no longer see the flashes of light. Above you towers Annapurna, with her white flanks of ice and snow. Then the sky lightens and the stars seem to disappear into the pale blue of the sky. Then sunlight bursts upon the peak of Machapuchhre. It seems to explode into gold and silver. Within minutes the light reaches Annapurna.

You stop for a cold breakfast of cheese and bread, washed down with tea, which you had brought along in jars.

Turn to page 112.

Click! The camera flashes with its battery-operated strobe.

Yikes! What a creature! It's really a Yeti! It has a huge, hairy body, a giant head, enormous feet. It is frightened by the strobe, and it spots you. It heads right for you, making awful sounds—half growl, half gurgle.

If you run for it, turn to page 36.

If you stay put, and fire the strobe light on the camera in hopes of scaring it off, turn to page 115.

You raise the ice ax. The Yeti, with eyes flashing, rips it from your hands, snaps it as though it were a twig, and hurls it over the cliff.

Then the Yeti speaks in controlled tones.

"Leave us in our homes. Your world has enough. If we wanted what you have, your cities, your crimes, your wars, we would join you. But we don't want these things. Leave us alone. This is a warning."

With that, the Yeti leaves. You stand and look at the fleeting figure. What will you tell the International Foundation For Research Into Strange Phenomena?

The End

You go on into the icefall. The sun turns the Khumbu Icefall into a giant solar furnace. You squint, even though you're wearing your dark glacier goggles. Your down parkas are stuffed in the rucksacks, and you are in shirtsleeves. Sirdar leads the way, cautiously skirting the huge, over-hanging blocks of ice, constantly probing the snow with his ice ax for a hidden crevasse—sure sign of a dangerous snow bridge.

You three are linked by a slender red-and-yellow rope that stretches between you.

Suddenly, with a whoop, three Yeti jump from their perch high above you, and push a giant ice block. It quivers, and then it begins to tumble, slowly at first, then it picks up speed as it rolls toward you. Other seracs start to tumble around you, and you are locked forever in a sea of ice.

You didn't even have a chance to see the Yeti. All that remains is their eerie cry, echoing in the ice-filled valley.

The End

"Let's think about it, Sirdar. The icefall is dangerous. The rains have weakened the ice and snow. Maybe it is a warning to us to leave this creature alone?"

Sirdar nods his head. "As you wish, bara sahib, as you wish."

That night, all your supplies mysteriously disappear. It is further warning to leave things as they are in these high mountains. The Yeti have their own way of life, and they do not want you—or anyone else—to disturb it.

The End

You walk out of the room. The Yeti, Zodak, accompanies you. Carlos stands outside, as he was when you left him. He is frozen in time. He can't hear you, nor can you hear him. You have become a part of a different world. You start to realize some of the consequences of your decision to go to Shangri-La.

You say a quiet goodbye to Carlos, even though he cannot hear you, and follow Zodak back into the monastery.

Go on to page 91.

Zodak motions to you to follow. He takes one giant step into the air. You look with amazement as he hovers a meter off the ground. Then you step up into the air, and you, too, are suspended above the floor of the monastery. You are levitating.

Whoosh!! The two of you zoom out of the monastery, right through the walls, up into the sky. You travel at unimaginable speeds. You climb at a dizzying pace, until the two of you stand on top of the sharp, icy crest of Mt. Everest. Below you stretch glaciers, mountains, valleys. You see the world from the top.

Zodak points to a narrow slot near the topmost point of Mt. Everest. He says, "That is the route to Shangri-La." He takes three steps, enters the slot, and disappears from sight.

Turn to page 96.

Runal backs away from the creature. You advance very quietly and ease the lens cap from your motor-driven camera.

You drop to one knee and position the camera, framing the Yeti and its meal against a backdrop of Lhotse and Everest.

Click—whiz—click. The motor drive is louder than you imagined. The Yeti stops eating; his head arches up and around. He sniffs the air. Then he sees you.

Turn to page 101.

It's probably the best decision to leave. Don't look for trouble. But what about Carlos?

You wait for his return, and you wait and wait and wait and wait. . . .

The End

"Back into the thicket! Hurry!"

You and Runal dart for it, and the Yeti is so busy eating that he pays no attention to the noises you two make.

"Now what? We can't go back that way, where the Yeti is, and we can't go deeper into this thicket where the others are."

As you finish speaking, the bushes in front of you are pushed aside. Three Yeti stand before you. The largest Yeti beckons you to follow. There is no choice but to do what he asks. The other two Yeti follow you and Runal. Any avenue of escape is cut off.

The pine and rhododendron bushes soon give way to a small clearing. At the far side is a smooth rock face perhaps a hundred meters high. On a group of boulders at the base of the rock sit a group of Yeti, varying in age and size. Carlos sits with them. He seems to be OK.

"Carlos! Hey, Carlos, what's happening?"

Carlos holds up his hand and says, "Listen to what they have to say."

Turn to page 106.

You take one last look at the Earth about you. You see the clouds rolling up from the flat, dry plains of the Punjab in India. You see the curve of the Earth. You see the contrail of an airplane far to the south.

Then you step into the narrow chute. It is warm, glistening with the shine of a metal unknown to you. You seem to hover in space in the narrow metal tube. But in truth you are moving at a great speed down through the center of Everest. There is a rose-colored glow around you.

Where is Zodak? Some guide, leaving you alone. What next?

Turn to page 99.

You feel confident that once you get to Carlos the two of you can plan an escape. The child, who is dressed in a dark maroon robe similar to that worn by Buddhist monks, leads you down into the valley. As if by magic, the valley appears as a city of light. Its radiance astounds you. Its brilliance dazzles but does not blind. Your fear fades.

Turn to page 108.

With a gentle bump, you come to rest. In front of you is a clear glass door. You push it open. There stands Zodak.

"Come. Welcome to Shangri-La."

You walk out into a dark green valley surrounded by lowlying hills. In the distance are high mountains. One of them looks like Everest. You hear music unlike any music you have ever heard before. It is somewhat like the sounds in the monastery, the bells and wind. The sunlight is warm and relaxing.

Zodak leads you down a long trail to a seven-story building. It seems to be a fortress, but it is painted white and red and gold. There are no soldiers, no guns, only people who smile and greet you as though you are an old friend.

It seems so natural. You turn to Zodak, and you get a shock. His form has changed. Now he is the mirror image of you! What does this mean?

Although you never find out about that, you learn about many things as you stay in the valley. You have the chance to try many activities you could never try before—but only what is available in the valley. You learn to be contented within the limits of the small valley.

Second thoughts?

Turn to page 107.

You and Carlos decide that it is too good an opportunity to pass up. You experience no fear or real hesitation. Maybe that has something to do with the light beam that seemed to wash away fear and doubt.

The head Movidian hovers near you. You even imagine that it is smiling, in spite of the fact that it has no face.

"What do we call you?" you ask. For a moment, there is just the humming of electrical circuits.

Then the Movidian answers, "You may call me Norcoon. I am an X52 Double L, intelligent, mobile activator being. I am head of this advance party. We will call you Earth One and Earth Two."

With a hiss, the creatures sink to the ground, where they sit and glow. Norcoon says, "Please, it is easier to travel to the Planet of the Seas in the Void of the Seven Moons if you remove your body and let your mind float free."

You look over at Carlos. What does this creature mean by "remove your body"?

"How? I mean, we are our bodies," says Carlos.

Norcoon points his light beam at you, and once again you feel the warmth and pleasure you felt before. Fear vanishes and, before you know it, you are free.

Turn to page 104.

You freeze. The camera slips out of your hands.

The Yeti jumps up with a roar and lunges at you. Before you know what has happened, the Yeti has you in its grasp.

Runal leaps forward, swinging the ice ax that he carries as a walking stick. He hits the Yeti three times on the shoulders with the flat face of the ax. The blows are as effective as a mosquito bite.

But then there is a sharp whistlelike call, and the Yeti suddenly drops you to the ground. You are shocked and unable to move.

The woman from the house appears.

Turn to page 105.

"No, we can't go. We must finish our expedition." You feel fear begin to creep back. You don't trust this thing.

Suddenly three Movidians turn on their light beams. Whammo! Carlos is hit with the beam, and he vanishes.

The head Movidian says, "Earth creature, don't be foolish. Join us. You will never regret it."

You start moving toward the side of the trail. No fast moves, just slow steps that don't seem to bother these strange creatures. You keep talking the entire time.

"Tell me more. I mean, what's it like up on the Planet of the Seas?"

"Oh, it is beautiful. You will like it. It is one of the higher realms. Only successful Earth creatures ever get to go there."

You ask, "What do you mean successful Earth creatures? What makes Carlos and me so successful?"

The Movidian glows a brighter color orange. You reach down, picking up a fist-sized rock, and, in a sweeping move, hurl it at the glowing blob. Just at that point, several Yeti come running up the trail. The Yeti are swinging great clubs. They slash rapidly in the air next to the Movidians, dodging the light beams. With a frantic gurgle, followed by a high-speed whoosh, the blobs depart.

Carlos reappears and, knowing the Yeti are now your allies, the two of you start to learn to communicate with them.

The End

Pure mind—no matter.

Norcoon approves, and offers you space aboard his mechanical transporter. Inside the pumpkin shape there is plenty of room for you and Carlos and all your thoughts.

"Now, my friends, we are on our way to the Planet of the Seas. It's where all thoughts end up."

You whirl away, confident that one day you will return wiser, and better able to help others in a world where the going is rough.

The End

The woman speaks rapidly in a tongue neither you nor Runal can understand. It is more a series of low grunts, mixed with high piercing whistles. The Yeti seems to become quiet, almost docile. Then the Yeti and the woman disappear into the thicket, leaving the two of you stunned and confused, but safe to return to Kathmandu with your pictures.

The End

You and Runal are made to sit in front of the group of Yeti. Your guards stand uneasily behind you. A Yeti of medium height, with a grayish tinge to his fur, stands and looks at you.

"You wanted to find us. Well, now you have. If you wish, take pictures. If you wish, record our voices. But listen well, listen and learn so that all will benefit."

His voice has a firm yet relaxed quality that erases your fear. Runal is actually smiling. Suddenly, it occurs to you that maybe he knew what was going on all the time.

The Yeti walks slowly around the circle of beings. He stops, looks to the sky and the mountains, and speaks.

Turn to page 111.

One last chance, is that it? Is that what you want? OK. You're on. Out of the valley of Shangri-La and back to the real world. Is it different? Can you do whatever you want? Can you fulfill your dreams? Can you enjoy your life completely? Or must you be content within limits?

The End

108

With gliding motions, you seem to fly along a pathway. It feels as though you have been there before.

"We are here. Please enter." The boy points the way to a building that seems to shimmer with inner light. It reminds you of the Taj Mahal, except it has many more towers, and the main dome is surrounded by hundreds of smaller domes, almost like leaves of a flower.

You take several steps forward, and then feel the grasping of a force not unlike magnetic force. You are held in the force field for several seconds, and then transported to the innermost room of the building.

Turn to page 59.

You huddle against the rock wall. The avalanche thunders by. Miraculously, you escape unharmed, except for choking on the snow crystals in the air.

Maybe you should get out now and go back to the red door.

Turn to page 82.

"In the beginning of time on this planet, life was difficult but simple. Survival was what held us together. We took the lives of only those things we needed to feed us. Nothing more."

A slight wind moves the branches of the pines. The Yeti continues his tale.

"Later, people found fire, lived in towns, made weapons, and killed one another. We, the Yeti, retreated, wanting none of the war nor the towns. We kept on retreating until there was no place left to go. So here we are, high in the mountains, where we thought we were safe."

"But you are safe. We mean no harm."

"Perhaps not you, but there are others who do. Leave us alone. Return to your own lands. If you want cities and war and this thing they call pollution, then live with them or get rid of them. But leave us be."

The group of Yeti nods in agreement. The meeting is over, and you, Carlos, and Runal are allowed to leave. You decide not to take pictures or record their voices. You also decide to suggest to the International Foundation For Research Into Strange Phenomena that a better study would be of the so-called civilized world.

The End

Soon you are at a vertical wall of rock. Above it you see the face of the ice. Carlos drives in a spike; you both rope up and proceed slowly up the rock.

Over the rock, you meet an expanse of firm snow. But under it lies hard, cold ice. On with the crampons. You lead the way, probing carefully with your ice ax to seek out any hidden crevasse.

The climb seems endless, and even though you are only five thousand meters up, the air is thin, and breathing is hard.

By mid-morning the sun is like a blast furnace. It reflects off the ice that surrounds you, and in the thin air the ultraviolet rays burn your skin. You both put white zinc ointment on your noses and lips.

Turn to page 114.

You had taken a sight bearing when you saw the flashes, but that was at night. Now, in daylight, it is not easy to be sure just where the flashes came from. But you have a good sense of direction, so you keep going.

Near noon, you gain a crest, and then you see it. It's a Pilatus Courier aircraft, one used for mountain flying. It lies in the snow, crumpled like a forgotten toy. The tail section is twisted, but the wings are intact. The engine is buried in the snow.

You both run to the plane, and open the cabin door. Huddled in the plane are the pilot and two passengers. One of the passengers is unconscious. You do what you can for the people; later that day a Royal Nepal Airlines helicopter finds you. All is well. It was the right thing to give help in the mountains. Congratulations for a job well done.

The End

Click! Click! You keep on flashing the strobe. The Yeti stops in its tracks, searches frantically for something, a friend perhaps, and then turns and, with amazing speed, vanishes into the night.

Unfortunately for you, you had *no* film in the camera.

The End

You look at Runal, you look at the monastery, you look at Carlos.

"No, I'm not ready to accept your offer."

No sooner have you spoken the words than clouds choke the narrow valley. The mountains seem to vanish, and the monastery is swallowed up by darkness. Runal turns his back to you and speaks as if to the wind.

"I am very sorry that you cannot accept. Since you do not feel that you can go ahead, the expedition is declared over. All permits are revoked. You must return to Kathmandu and leave the country in twenty-four hours."

The note of finality in Runal's voice tells you that you have no choice whatsoever. Your trip is over.

The End

ABOUT THE AUTHOR

R. A. MONTGOMERY is an educator and publisher. A graduate of Williams College, he also studied in graduate programs at Yale University and New York University. After serving in a variety of administrative capacities at Williston Academy and Columbia University, he co-founded the Waitsfield Summer School in 1965. Following that, Montgomery helped found a research and development firm specializing in the development of educational programs. He worked for several years as a consultant to the Peace Corps in Washington, D.C. and West Africa. He is now both a writer and a publisher.

ABOUT THE ILLUSTRATOR

PAUL GRANGER is a prize-winning illustrator and painter.

CHOOSE YOUR OWN ADVENTURE ®

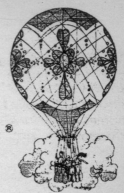

You'll want all the books in the exciting *Choose Your Own Adventure*® series offering you hundreds of fantasy adventures without ever leaving your chair. Each book takes you through an adventure—under the sea, in a space colony, on a volcanic island—in which you become the main character. What happens next in the story depends on the choices *you* make and *only you* can decide how the story ends!

☐	23228	THE CAVE OF TIME #1 Edward Packard	$1.95
☐	23229	JOURNEY UNDER THE SEA #2 R. A. Montgomery	$1.95
☐	23183	BY BALLOON TO THE SAHARA #3 D. Terman	$1.95
☐	23180	SPACE AND BEYOND #4 R. A. Montgomery	$1.95
☐	23184	THE MYSTERY OF CHIMNEY ROCK #5 Edward Packard	$1.95
☐	23182	YOUR CODE NAME IS JONAH #6 Edward Packard	$1.95
☐	23185	THE THIRD PLANET FROM ALTAIR #7 Edward Packard	$1.95
☐	23230	DEADWOOD CITY #8 Edward Packard	$1.95
☐	23181	WHO KILLED HARLOWE THROMBEY? #9 Edward Packard	$1.95
☐	23231	THE LOST JEWELS OF NABOOTI #10 R. A. Montgomery	$1.95
☐	23186	MYSTERY OF THE MAYA #11 R. A. Montgomery	$1.95
☐	23175	INSIDE UFO 54-40 #12 Edward Packard	$1.95
☐	23332	THE ABOMINABLE SNOWMAN #13 R. A. Montgomery	$1.95
☐	23236	THE FORBIDDEN CASTLE #14 Edward Packard	$1.95
☐	22541	HOUSE OF DANGER #15 R. A. Montgomery	$1.95
☐	22768	SURVIVAL AT SEA #16 Edward Packard	$1.95
☐	23290	THE RACE FOREVER #17 Ray Montgomery	$1.95
☐	23292	UNDERGROUND KINGDOM #18 Edward Packard	$1.95